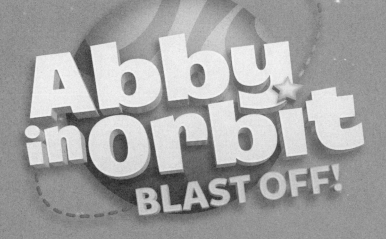

Abby in Orbit
BLAST OFF!

Andrea J. Loney

illustrated by Fuuji Takashi

Albert Whitman & Company
Chicago, Illinois

For my mom, Phyllis, the most brilliant star
in my universe—AJL

To my dear Father, through whom all
dreams become possible—FT

Library of Congress Cataloging-in-Publication data is on file with the publisher.

Text copyright © 2022 by Andrea J. Loney

Illustrations copyright © 2022 by Albert Whitman & Company

Illustrations by Fuuji Takashi

First published in the United States of America in 2022 by Albert Whitman & Company

ISBN 978-0-8075-0099-6 (hardcover)

ISBN 978-0-8075-0100-9 (ebook)

Printed in the United States of America

10 9 8 7 6 5 4 3 2 1 LB 26 25 24 23 22

Design by Aphelandra

For more information about Albert Whitman & Company,
visit our website at www.albertwhitman.com.

Contents

Abby's Orbit

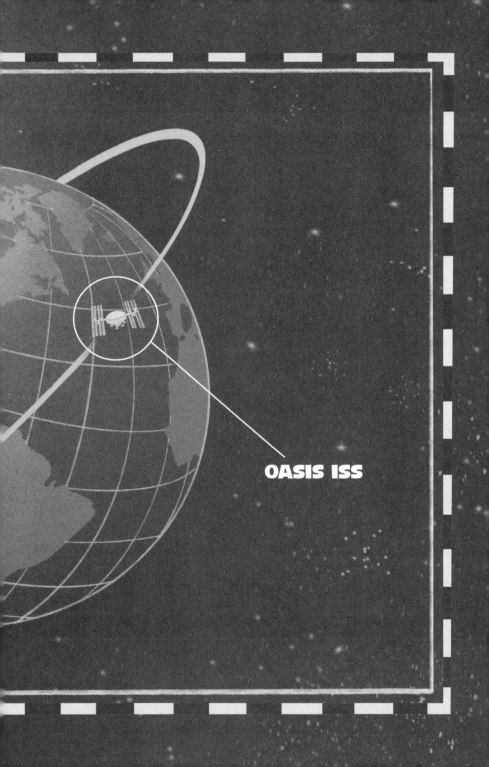

CHAPTER 1

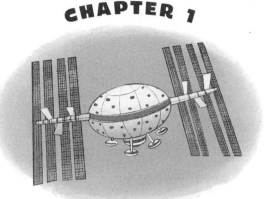

Out of This World

"Abby? Are you listening to me?" Mami asked as she snapped the barrette on the end of my braid.

"Yes, Mami!" I said, even if it wasn't 100 percent, completely, all-the-way true since I was still watching my new tablet. Yes, it was turned off, but it was floating in the air, spinning right in front of me.

We'd only been on the space station for a few days. I wasn't used to microgravity. Papa said it's way less gravity than there is on Earth but a tiny bit more gravity than there is on the moon. I just thought it was out-of-this-world amazing and eleventy-seventy kinds of cool.

"Things are sooooo different here," I said.

Mami sighed and shook her head. Her swirly, curly crown of black hair looked even more amazing in space.

"Wow, Mami, you're like the queen of the universe."

Mami turned to Papa. "Jeremiah, please talk to this child. I need to see if NASA updated the coordinates for today's experiment." She stretched out her tablet and started typing.

"So, Abby." The twinkle in Papa's eye meant a big fat pun was coming. "Why did the little astronaut get in trouble at school?"

I knew that one. "Because she kept spacing out!"

"That's my girl!" Papa laughed. "You're ready for the third grade."

But was I? Things were so different. Last year Nico and I still went to school on Earth with school buses, cupcakes, and rain puddles on the playground. There were crayons. There was gravity. But none of that existed on the international space station, OASIS.

All last year our whole family was far, far apart. Mami was running a big project up here on the OASIS. Papa was programming 3D-printing labs on the moon. My little brother, Nico, and I stayed in Houston with Nana Sherry and her yappy little dog who hates kids. Then they opened the new Schoolhouse Academy on the OASIS, so our family was finally back together again.

At least for now.

"I think I'm ready, Papa, I just—"

"*¡Mira!* Take my picture, Mami!" Nico somersaulted in the air, then whirled to a stop. Upside down. With his feet in my face.

"Eww! Nico!" His socks smelled like sweat and peppermint. Who gets toothpaste on their toes?

I double-checked my shirt to make sure it was tucked into my pants all the way around—no rainbow stars peeking out the back. Even if they were my lucky undies, I wanted to look like a serious big-kid third grader, not a silly little second grader. But I still had lots of big second-grader feelings inside.

It's hard to keep it all together when things keep floating away.

"Well," Mami said with a shrug, "here's our first day of school, fall 2051."

Spending my first day of third grade with

my whole family on the OASIS was my biggest wish-upon-a-star, win-the-lottery dream come true.

I wasn't going to let anything ruin that for us, not even Nico's feet.

"You'll see!" I said, "I'll be the most organized, dependable, mature kid on the whole space station and—"

Bonk! My floating tablet smacked Papa right on his shiny, bald head. I snatched it from the air and hid it under my arm.

"Sorry, Papa," I said.

"Aww, Moon Drop," he said, "don't worry. We know you'll make us proud."

Mami put my tablet on the charging pad with hers.

"Now, listen to your teacher today," Mami said. "Take a breath and think before you act. Make good choices."

I nodded, not just hearing her this time, but using my super, strongest focus powers to really listen. Although 5 percent of me was still thinking about decorating my plain old tablet with rainbow-star stickers.

"I'm running an important experiment today, Abby. We're livestreaming to universities all over the world—even to deep space. So keep an eye on your brother and be on your best behavior while I'm at work."

Mami and I didn't always agree on what "best behavior" really meant. I meant that I always tried my best, but sometimes I still behaved myself into all kinds of trouble. Papa said it was part of my big personality. But I couldn't risk Mami sending us back to Earth.

Nico never worried about anything. He was busy headbutting his inflatable soccer ball, even though we had to leave soon.

Mami and Papa didn't even notice. They were busy discussing Mami's big experiment again. I didn't really understand much, but it had something to do with super-cold atoms, neutron stars, and new galaxies. Mami liked big, complicated ideas the size of the universe. Papa liked how the tiny details all fit together. I liked the way they smiled at each other.

Instead of battling Nico, I packed our bags for school. Squeezy mango fruit packets. Water packets too. Peanut butter and jelly in tortillas, since breadcrumbs could mess up the air system. I put Nico's tablet in his bag, but the rest were still charging. Then I made my last trip to the bathroom so I wouldn't have to figure out some weird plumbing system at school.

I was finally ready.

"Okay, Baxters," Mami said as she flew past me to grab her tablet from the charger. "*¡Vamos! Let's go!*"

Papa took my hand. "Time to blast off."

On the way to the door, I took the last tablet and popped it into my backpack.

I was ready to leave our cozy family space-station pod with its tiny eating, sleeping, and potty quarters. I was ready for the third grade in the OASIS Schoolhouse Academy. I was ready to be focused and responsible.

"C'mon, Nico," I said, reaching for his sticky little hand.

I turned.

Behind me the soccer ball twirled alone in the empty capsule. Nico had disappeared. Again.

"Cheese and craters!" I said with a moan.

Maybe I wasn't 100 percent ready after all.

CHAPTER 2

Countdown to Third Grade

The heavy metal-and-glass door *shuuushed* closed behind me. I entered the bright metal corridor, far behind my parents. But where was Nico?

A giggle. Toothpaste toes. Nico twirled right over my head.

"Abby, get your brother and let's go!"

As Nico and I reached the big oval door at the end of the corridor, Mami turned and smiled. Just seeing the pride in her eyes made me smile too.

"Welcome to the OASIS, kids," Mami said.

The doorway *shussshed* open. Suddenly we were in the middle of a huge, noisy, open pod the size of a school gymnasium. People flowed above us, below us, and all around, speaking languages I'd never heard before. They came from countries all over the world, the lunar station, and even the new station on Mars. They popped in and out of oval doorways that hissed open and closed.

"This is the Main Pod," Papa said. "Most of the other pods branch off from here. School's over there."

I tried to follow Papa's finger, but I still couldn't get over all our new neighbors. Who were these people? How would I remember all their names?

"Good morning, Dr. Baxter!" Someone waved at Mami. My mother nodded back.

"Hey, Doc B!" a man said to Papa with a fist bump. Everyone seemed to know Mami and Papa.

Finally we reached the big oval doorway marked SCHOOLHOUSE in bright blue letters.

"I need to set up the data links in the lab." Mami checked her watch. "But you'll both be fine." She kissed the top of Nico's head. Then she straightened the collar of my school uniform. "Now go in there and make me proud, *mi corazón*."

Watching how other people looked at my parents with respect and admiration made me extra proud to be a Baxter. It was time to be the best third grader ever.

Papa gave Mami a kiss. Then he pulled hard on the latch until the door to the school pod corridor *creaaaked* open.

"Hmm...They should fix that door so it doesn't stick," Mami said. She floated off.

"Okay, Baxters." Papa hooked his arms in ours. "The kindergarten and third-grade dual launch commences in..."

Papa, Nico, and I zipped through the shiny hall as we counted down together.

"Ten, nine, eight, seven, six, five, four, three, two, one!"

The classroom door swung open.

So did my mouth.

"CHEESE AND CRATERS!" I shouted.

The OASIS schoolhouse was another pod, the size of a regular classroom. But this pod was filled with kids! Little kids not much older than Nico. Big teenagers. And everyone else was somewhere in between.

But the biggest, wackiest, most brain-twisty part?

They were everywhere! Sideways on the walls, doing classwork! Upside-down on the ceiling, reading their tablets! Stretched out on the floor, drawing on a big screen!

And there I was, spinning around to see everything and everyone. I was so confused! I was 350 percent not ready for this!

"Hey, look," some big kid whispered from one of the pod walls. "Are those rainbow-star underpants?"

I looked behind me. All my twisting and turning had untucked my shirt.

"What a baby!" someone else whispered. Then some kids started giggling.

Then Papa whispered something in my ear, but I was too upset to hear it. This was not how I meant to start the third grade. This was not how I wanted to make my mark on the OASIS.

And Nico was even more offended than I was.

"No, no, no!" Nico waved his finger at the other kids. "My big sister, Abby, is *not* a baby! I am the baby! Me!"

Then there was more laughter—but the good kind. I laughed along with everyone else. A few kids came over to meet us.

"He's so cute!"

"Look at this little guy!"

Nico grinned and spun and posed for his new fans. And I tucked my shirt back in.

Our new teacher floated over to us. He had shiny black hair, warm brown skin, elbow patches on his old-timey jacket, and the kind of smile that instantly made me feel at home.

"Doc B," the man said in a crisp booming voice. "How wonderful to meet you and your progeny!"

"Progeny"? What was that? Something you see a doctor about?

"Mr. Krishna," Papa said, "my progeny can't wait to join your class. Right, kids?"

Oh, *we* were the progeny. Nico and I nodded.

"Okay, Baxters." Papa put his arms around our shoulders. "I'm heading to the shop to code some new models. Be good. And if you can't be good…"

"Be awesome!" Nico and I whispered together, giggling.

"Don't tell your mother I taught you that." He gave us a big hug before he left.

Then it was just me, Nico, and a huge whirling cube of floating classmates.

How was I supposed to focus on anything?

CHAPTER 3

The One Pod Schoolhouse

Mr. Krishna quickly explained the OASIS One Pod Schoolhouse. There were only thirteen kids on the space station, so he split us into four groups—kindergarten to first grade, second grade to fourth grade, fifth grade to seventh grade, and eighth grade to high school. Every hour the groups swapped activity stations, so all the students could spend time reading and writing, exercising, learning math and science, talking about intergalactic social studies, and making music and art.

When we first showed up, three Level 1 kids were on the port wall (Mr. Krishna liked to use astronaut terms based on where the space station was facing, and that one meant the left side), two Level 2 kids were on the stern wall (the right side), three Level 3 kids were on the ceiling (overhead), and three Level 4 kids were on the floor (the deck). Mr. Krishna's control station was on the aft wall (the back), but he mostly stayed in the middle, floating from one group to another.

As soon as Mr. Krishna mentioned the Level 1 station, Nico zoomed off to join his classmates. In seconds he and his new friends were laughing and playing.

"And Abby, you'll be joining Gracie and Dmitry here in Level 2. Gracie's also in the third grade." Mr. Krishna pointed to a girl with a neat black bob who was drawing the sun on the big screen. She seemed so small compared to her awesome artwork. And she didn't look up at all.

This was it. I'd finally made it to the third grade. I was 115 percent ready to do mature third-grade things and have mature third-grade conversations about...well, I wasn't exactly sure, but I was excited to find out.

I floated over. Gracie just kept drawing.

"So you're Gracie, right?" I said, hoping she'd respond before the end of the school year.

"Yes," the girl finally said, peeking at me through her bangs. "Gracie Chen."

Gracie looked around at the other kids for a moment. Then she leaned close to me.

"I have a secret to tell you," she whispered in my ear. "I like rainbow stars."

"They're my favorite!" I said in relief.

"Mine too!" Gracie replied, this time with a smile that lit up her whole face.

Level 2 was working on a diagram of the solar system. Gracie had already finished the sun and Mercury, and she was starting on Venus. She made drawing look so easy.

"Maybe you could start with Earth?" Gracie asked.

"Earth is my favorite!" I said with a fancy spin that made Gracie look down and hide her face again. So then I quietly sketched my all-time favorite planet on the digital screen. A little blue for the oceans, a little green for the continents, and then—

"That is all wrong."

An older boy floated behind me with his arms crossed. His uniform was spotless, his shiny brown hair was perfectly gelled, and his sharp eyes glared right at me.

"South America is too big here. And you are supposed to use a stylus, not your fingers. And—"

"Dmitry," Gracie said softly, "it's only her first day."

But as he drew Mars and Jupiter, Dmitry kept complaining that I was destroying the galaxy. And I was getting mad.

"Are you making our new friend comfortable, Level 2?" Mr. Krishna looked right at Dmitry.

"She has no idea what she is doing," Dmitry grumbled.

"That is 100 percent true," I said. "But you

don't have to say it like that."

"I see," said Mr. Krishna as Dmitry and I fumed at each other.

Mr. Krishna turned to the whole class. "OASIS schoolhouse scholars, may I have your attention?"

"Yes, Mr. Krishna," the students said in unison.

We all floated to the center to surround him. Mr. Krishna opened his hand, and a hologram of Earth popped up. As the hologram spun on his palm, Mr. Krishna called out each continent and asked the students who were born there to raise their hands. He and some students raised their hands for Asia. Dmitry and some others raised their hands for Europe. Gracie, Nico, and I all raised our hands high for North America. Other students raised their hands for Africa, South America, and Australia. Then

Mr. Krishna asked everyone from planet Earth to raise their hands. All hands went up.

"Remember," Mr. Krishna said, "you, your parents, and everyone here on the OASIS is a part of one big team. None of us live here alone. Everything we do affects everyone else. We must all succeed or fail together, so we must all learn how to work together."

I thought about how everyone in the room, and on the international space station, and on Earth, the moon, and Mars, and even on ships in space, were all part of the same team. It made me feel warm and tingly inside.

Ding!

The students all rushed back to their stations and started packing up their things.

"What's going on?" I asked.

"Time for reading," Gracie said. She saved the file on the screen.

Another *ding*. The students launched themselves across the pod to rotate stations. I bounced into at least three other kids as I followed Gracie to the next station.

The reading station was just a small screen with some instructions:

Level 2: 3rd graders read pages 104–107
4th graders read pages 206–217

WELCOME, READERS

Dmitry had already looped himself into a harness on the wall so he could read his tablet without floating around.

"He'll be quiet now," Gracie said. "You'll see."

Gracie pulled her tablet from her backpack and smiled at me. Maybe things would be okay after all.

I made a checklist in my mind of all the things I needed to learn:

1) How to float better

2) How to be a better third grader so Dmitry won't yell at me, even though he's

   a) already a fourth grader,

   b) 90 percent mean, and

   c) 200 percent too picky

3) How to stay focused in the One Pod Schoolhouse

It felt like a lot. But really it was only three things. I could do three things.

I reached into my backpack and pulled out my tablet. But something about it was weird.

"Is everything all right, Abby?" Gracie asked.

Dmitry glanced up from his tablet, so I quickly nodded yes. And I pretended to be reading even though

I wasn't. Okay, that part was not 100 percent true. I was reading the screen. A big blinky alert said:

PROPERTY OF DR. SILVIA BAXTER.
AUTHORIZATION DENIED.

I'd taken Mami's tablet instead of mine. The tablet she needed for her big experiment. I was in so much trouble. I was in a world, a galaxy, a universe of trouble.

And so was Mami.

CHAPTER 4

Houston,
We Have a Problem

I had to find Mami. I had to get this tablet back in her hands and out of mine. But how?

My heart thumped so loud and so fast I was sure the whole One Pod Schoolhouse could hear it. My eyes felt hot and blurry. But no one seemed to notice. Gracie and Dmitry quietly read their tablets. The rest of the students worked on their projects. Even Nico was busy drawing on the big screen with the other Level 1 kids.

So I pretended I was working too. I looked down at Mami's tablet. There was the reflection of my own worried, frowny face. Craters!

Could I ask Mr. Krishna for help? He and the Level 4 students were having a serious grown-up discussion. I'd feel like a whiny little kid asking him to help me find my mommy.

I had to figure this out on my own. But how? When was the last time I found something I was looking for?

"Um, Abby," Gracie whispered, "it might be easier to read the story if you turn your tablet on."

"I can't…" I was almost afraid to even tell Gracie. "See?"

I showed her the screen. Gracie's mouth and eyes opened wide with shock.

"Cheese and craters, Abby!" Gracie covered her mouth. "Wow—I never said that before. It's kinda fun."

"This is reading time," Dmitry said without looking up from his tablet, "not chatting time!"

"I have to get this back to my mother right now," I told Gracie. "But I don't know where her lab is."

"I think I know who does," Gracie said. She took off across the room.

"Yes!" Just hearing Gracie's words made me feel 150 percent better.

Across the pod, Gracie was talking with a tall girl with a long black French braid in Level 3. She pointed at me, then they flew back together.

"This is my big sister, Claire," Gracie said.

"You're Dr. Baxter's kid?"

"Uh, yeah."

"Really?" Claire said with a frown. "I guess I expected someone more…organized. Anyway, Gracie's got the directions now."

Claire gave me one more disappointed look, then left.

"Um, thanks?"

"Don't mind her," Gracie said. "She just turned twelve, so now she's like that to everyone."

Ding!

This was our chance! While everyone was changing stations, we'd zip out the door, get the tablet to Mami, and be back before anyone noticed.

"Let's go, Gracie!" I said.

"Sure, we'll just tell Mr. Krishna that—"

"No!" I didn't want anyone else to know. I didn't want anyone else judging me. I just wanted to fix the problem.

"We'll be right back," I said to Gracie. "Let's just go."

"Go where?" Dmitry asked. "It is time for exercise."

Ding!

The students flew to their next stations. I headed for the door, but Gracie pulled me to the exercise station instead.

"But—" I protested.

"Shh!"

The exercise station had three stationary bikes with harnesses, virtual reality goggles, and gloves.

"Ha! I can beat you both!" Dmitry crowed

as he strapped himself into the bike and slid on his goggles. Then he played a virtual reality game while he pedaled.

"You're too fast for us, Dmitry." Gracie gave me a sly smile. Then she mouthed the words, "Let's go."

As the rest of the students found their stations, Gracie and I slipped through the big oval door. The quiet of the empty corridor felt so good after the noisiness of the school pod. I could breathe better. I could focus.

"So where are we going?" I asked.

Gracie brought up a hand-sketched map on her tablet. "This is the fastest route from here."

It looked like a bunch of pipes and tubes to me. But I trusted her. We'd follow the map, switch the tablets, and scoot back in no time.

Ugh! Gracie and I both had to pull hard on the latch to open the big door at the end of the corridor. Then we were back in the busy Main Pod.

"You are not supposed to be out here!"

We turned. Still wearing virtual reality goggles on his forehead, Dmitry scowled at us both.

"This is personal business," I replied. Gracie nodded.

"I'm telling Mr. Krishna!" Dmitry shouted. He turned to open the door back to the school pod, but it was stuck again.

"They really need to fix that," I said. "C'mon, Gracie."

We headed across the Main Pod.

"You can't leave me out here!" Dmitry shouted. "Wait for meeeee!"

CHAPTER 5

Sticking to the Plan

At first I tried to lose Dmitry. That boy had "tattletale" written all over his face. Then I thought about what Mr. Krishna said about us all being a team, succeeding or failing together. And even though I didn't like the things Dmitry said or the way he said them, I still had to learn how to work with him.

So I stopped, turned, and forced a smile.

"C'mon, Dmitry."

As the grown-ups rushed past us, Gracie and I explained the situation.

"You took your mother's tablet?" Dmitry laughed. "What a dum-dum!"

I knew we should've left him behind.

"Mr. Krishna says that word is not constructive," Gracie told Dmitry as she put her arm around my shoulder. "You can do better."

Dmitry thought for a moment, looking a little guilty.

"*Da*, Gracie." Then Dmitry turned to me. "We all make mistakes sometimes. Some of us more than others, Abby."

I guess that was the Dmitry version of an apology, but it barely made me feel 25 percent better.

Following the map on Gracie's tablet, we crossed the Main Pod with a dozen other people, sailed past the living quarters, and entered the portal door to the work pods. The first laboratory pod had a skinny observation window at the top. On the inside of the pod, scientists ran experiments with test tubes, microscopes, and even lab mice. In the hallway outside the pod, a few other scientists watched through the glass and made notes on their tablets.

"Wow! That's out of this world!" I whispered to Gracie.

"Technically," Dmitry said, "everything on the OASIS is out of the world. The world is over there."

He pointed to a window near the end of the pod. Through it I could just make out a small blue marble—planet Earth. Just as I tried to float closer to the window—

"And where are you children going?" A man in a uniform stopped us.

We all looked at each other. Dmitry adjusted his VR goggles.

"Um, we're going to see my dad in his shop," I said confidently.

"Oh, you must be Doc B's daughter. We heard about you."

The man chuckled and floated off.

"That was scary!" Gracie shivered. "We could have gotten caught."

"You are a surprisingly good liar," Dmitry said with a grin.

Ugh. That was *not* how I wanted to impress Dmitry. I didn't mean to lie. The words just shot out of my mouth. And it was only 50 percent of a lie, because I really did want to find my dad and see if he could help me fix this. I wasn't lying, I was wishing.

Still, I wished I hadn't said it. Now I was a tablet snatcher and a fibber.

"I just want to get this tablet to my mom," I said. "What if she can't start her experiment without it? What if she gets in trouble? What if she sends me back to live with Nana Sherry and her yappy little dog who hates kids?"

Gracie took my arm. "We're almost there, Abby. No need to worry about that zappy dog."

"Zappy?" I said. "No, yappy."

"Oh," Gracie said, "I thought your grandmother had a broken robot dog!"

Now I couldn't stop thinking about a messed-up robot version of Nana Sherry's dog. It made me giggle.

Suddenly Gracie flattened herself against the wall with a squeak. She pulled the rest of us back too.

"What's going on?" I whispered. "Is someone after us? Are we under attack? Did something escape from the lab?"

"Worse," Gracie whispered back. She pointed at a scientist zipping down the corridor. He wore lab goggles and studied his tablet without even looking up. His nose and chin looked a lot like Gracie's and Claire's.

"My *baba*," Gracie whispered. "If he saw me here, I would be in so much trouble."

"That's your dad? He looks really, um, intense."

"He's always like that."

"Just like my mami."

"My papa too," Dmitry added.

We all sighed, even Dmitry. It didn't always feel 100 percent great to have a super intense mom or dad. But it felt at least 75 percent better to know that someone else felt the same way.

"We have to be more careful," I said. "Let's do this and rush right back."

CHAPTER 6

The Great Switcheroo

"This is it!" Gracie double-checked her tablet.

We floated before a narrow passageway with a door to another pod on the left side. Along the top left wall of the passageway was a long, narrow window. There was another door at the far end of the passageway.

"Yes, this is the big lab," Dmitry said.

We pulled ourselves up the wall. Then we peered through the observation window.

But to be 100 percent honest, I didn't want to look. What if Mami was angry that I took her tablet?

What if she was telling the other scientists how unfocused I was? Or worse yet, what if the other scientists thought Mami was unfocused? What if they got so mad at Mami they kicked her off the OASIS?

I had to fix this. I peered through the window with Gracie and Dmitry. Mami was talking to two other scientists. They all worked on a big screen filled with data and video models.

"It looks like they are still setting up," Dmitry said.

"Do you see the tablet?" Gracie asked.

I pulled myself closer to the window. There were hooks, loops, and gadgets all over the room. And then—there, on the far end of the room, hooked to a Velcro strap on the wall, was Mami's bag. My tablet floated inside of it.

"Yes! It's right there!"

"Good," Gracie said. "So let's go in there and—"

"No, no, NO!" I yanked Gracie down from the window. "Mami cannot know that I'm not in school right now. And she can't know that I took her tablet."

I peeked in the window again. Mami had on her happy focused face—her eyes were shining, and everyone was listening to her. I couldn't mess that up.

"I have to sneak in and swap the tablets."

"How?" Gracie asked.

"Well, Mami's bag is all the way on that side of the pod, but the screen is right here. If they're all looking this way, maybe they won't even see me over there."

"So you have eyes on the back of your head?" Dmitry asked. "How will you know where they are looking?"

The answer blasted into my brain like a rocket.

"You two brought your tablets, right? Dmitry, do you have earphones?"

He nodded.

"I do too." Gracie pulled her earphones from her bag.

"Can you set up a voice chat from tablet to tablet?"

"Of course I can! What do you think I am, a third grader?" Dmitry took out his tablet and called Gracie's.

Chirp!

Gracie jabbed the volume button on her tablet.

"Oops!" she squeaked.

"Someone's coming!" Dmitry said as he peeked through the window. His words came through the earphones in Gracie's hand.

"Cool," said Gracie, handing me her earphones.

"Now I get it," Dmitry said as I popped Gracie's earphones into my hopefully 90 percent–clean ears. "We will be like mission control on the ground!"

"And you'll be like an astronaut on a spacewalk!" Gracie said.

Yes! They were on board with my plan! I wanted to spin with joy, but we had to move fast. So I happy-danced for just a second in my mind.

It was Gracie's idea to knock on the door. Then, when the scientist came to open it, we hid on the ceiling. He didn't think to look up.

"You are clear for takeoff!" I could hear Dmitry's voice in my earphones as he watched everyone through the high lab window. Gracie stuck her foot at the top of the door before it closed. There was just enough space for me to float in, silent and slow. Without the micro-gravity, I 100 percent would have banged into something.

"Get up against the wall," Dmitry said, "and wait for them to change the screen again."

I leaned back, holding my breath. My heart pounded. Now Mami was spinning a huge hologram of an atom in her palm. One scientist poked at the hologram and spun it. The other scientist kept asking Mami questions. I think she was Mami's new assistant. What was her name again? It was one of those old-timey names like Nevaeh, or Rihanna...

"Why do you sit there like a stone?" growled Dmitry. "Now! Go, go, go!"

Quickly and carefully, I crawled to Mami's bag. And just as I went to open it—

"Wait!" Dmitry said.

On the other side of the pod, Mami showed everyone a huge hologram of a crystal. The scientists got excited again.

"Now!" Dmitry said.

Quickly, I ripped the Velcro tab open like pulling off a Band-Aid. No one heard me. I swapped the tablets and hugged mine to my chest. I was so happy I wanted to dance again, but now I had to get back out.

Gracie's foot was still in the doorway.

"Now?" I whispered to Dmitry.

"Wait…wait…*now*!"

Mami turned back to the big screen. Both holograms danced on the screen. The scientists started chattering again. I slipped out without anyone noticing me.

We did it!

Gracie and I joined Dmitry at the observation window.

"Mission accomplished!" said Dmitry.

He even smiled.

"Cheese and craters!" Gracie said, her cheeks rosy with excitement. "That was out of this world, Abby!"

"I told you," Dmitry said. "We are *already* out of the world. That is just a regular day here on the OASIS."

"So what's even bigger and farther than out

of this world?" Gracie asked.

"That was *interstellar*!" I said.

"I love it!" Gracie replied.

"What do you think, Dmitry?"

Dmitry zoomed past us to the other end of the corridor.

"I think we should get out of here before they catch us!"

We barely squeezed through the door before we heard a man's voice.

"Did you hear that? It sounded like children."

"It's time to start," boomed Mami's voice. "I'll get my tablet."

CHAPTER 7

Cosmic Catastrophe

The next corridor was much darker than the one by the lab, and a little spooky. But I was so happy, I didn't care. I was too busy doing my happy dance and singing.

Interstellar! Interstellar!
Abby, Gracie, and Dmitry—
We're I-N-T-E-R-S-T-E-L-L-A-R!
I say 'inter'!

You say 'stellar'!

Inter—

—stellar!

Inter—

—stellar!

Gracie and I laughed. But Dmitry frowned and pointed to a sign over my head. The words were in Russian.

"Abby, watch out!" he yelled.

Too late. Turns out I'd danced right into a restricted part of the pod.

Braaap! Braaaap! Braaaaap!

Red lights flashed. The loudest, ugliest alarm I'd ever heard blared and screeched.

"What do we do?" Gracie asked, terrified.

"Let's go that way!" I said in a panic.

The door at the end of the hall led to another large area like the Main Pod. Scientists, workers, and other people rushed around. A uniformed man with a light stick waved everyone to the

back of the pod.

"This way! This way!" said the man.

"Do not look at anyone," Dmitry said. "Do not talk to anyone. Just blend in and be quiet."

It didn't work.

"Hey, shouldn't you be in school?" The man pointed his light stick at us.

He'd caught us trying to hide behind the others. He slowly raised his watch and spoke into it, never taking his eyes off of us.

It would have been the perfect time for a black hole to swallow us up. But no such luck.

"This is *not* interstellar, Abby," Dmitry muttered.

Finally the alarms and the red lights stopped. The pod was completely, mute-button silent. We stood waiting.

Then everyone turned as a small woman parted the crowd. Her uniform glittered with shiny medals on the front and sparkly patches on the shoulders. She looked over everyone and didn't smile. Then she saw us at the back of the room. She raised one eyebrow.

My hands started sweating.

"Commander Johansson," Dmitry whispered. "She is the big boss of the OASIS."

Everyone was scared of her. I was too. But I had to explain what happened.

Gracie and Dmitry tried to stop me.

"No, Abby!" said Gracie.

"*Nyet!*" added Dmitry. "You will make things worse!"

"Good morning, Commander Johansson." I reached out for a handshake. She looked down at my hand like it was a crumpled piece of paper.

"Abigail Baxter," the commander said in a voice much deeper than I expected. "The oldest child of Dr. Silvia Baxter and Dr. Jeremiah Baxter. You are—" She squinted like I was a glitch on a screen. "—not at all what I expected."

I didn't like how her words felt in my heart.

"Dmitry Petrov? Gracie Chen?"

"Yes, Commander Johansson!" they said at the same time.

"I did not expect to find either of you in this situation. All of your parents have been notified."

Gracie's cheeks flushed bright red. Dmitry's face turned as white as the moon. Neither of them said a word.

"But it's not their fault," I said. Gracie,

Dmitry, and even some of the grown-ups shook their heads, but that only made me talk faster.

"You see," I told the commander, "I took the wrong tablet, and I was just trying to bring back the right one, and it was only supposed to take a few minutes, but we went the wrong way, and we would have gone straight back to class, and okay, maybe I danced a little too much, but I only wanted to celebrate our mission accomplished, and my friends shouldn't get in trouble for that and—"

Commander Johansson just stared at me. She said nothing. It felt like she was looking straight through me.

And then, out of nowhere, it happened. Tears oozed from my eyes, and the room got swirly, and I couldn't stop it.

"Abby!" I heard Gracie and Dmitry yelling. "Abby, don't cry!"

But I couldn't help it. All the feelings I'd tried to hold in for the whole day just poured out of my face. Well, they didn't exactly "pour."

Here's a really important fact about crying on the OASIS: In space, tears don't run down your cheeks. They don't fall at all. They just... bubble up into these big, goopy, salty snot-

balls that cover your whole face. And then you can't breathe, and you look like a big slimy-headed monster. I don't rec-ommend it.

"Abby, nooooo!" Gracie said.

"Calm down!" Dmitry yelled.

And I wanted to stop. I really did. Then it got worse.

Hic!

Hic! Hic! HIC!

Sometimes too much crying gives me the hiccups.

Adults crowded around to make sure I was okay. Someone handed Gracie a towel to help me mop up all the goo. Dmitry patted my back really hard, which didn't help at all.

Commander Johansson just turned and headed to the door.

"Children, follow me. Now."

CHAPTER 8

The Big Eclipse

Hic!

The trip back to school happened in a flash. Aside from my hiccups, none of us said anything as we followed Commander Johansson. But the closer we got to the class, the louder my heart pounded, and then—

"Abby!"

My mother's voice scared me so much I thought my hiccups might stop.

"Yes, Mami? *Hic!*"

Nope.

Everyone in the One Pod Schoolhouse just stopped and stared at us. And not just the kids—our parents were waiting too!

Mami glared at me with her hands on her hips and one eyebrow raised high. I was in so much trouble.

Hic! Hic!

Mr. Krishna floated over to us and smiled. "Oh look, Level 2 is back from an unscheduled field trip. I see you brought Commander Johansson…here…to my classroom."

His smile looked a lot less happy.

"Grace?" said a woman who looked a lot like Gracie and Claire, especially her eyes and cheeks.

"Dmitry," growled a stony-faced man with a mustache. He looked like a bigger, older, meaner version of Dmitry.

Gracie and Dmitry both looked ready to cry.

"Look," I said to all the adults, "I made a mistake—no, I made a lot of mistakes. I'm sorry I took the wrong tablet. I'm sorry I got Gracie and Dmitry and—"

Gracie's big sister, Claire, glared at me as I almost said her name.

Hic! Whew! Saved by the hiccup.

"I'm sorry I got us all in this mess."

Then I turned to Mami and Papa. Looking into my mother's eyes was 250 percent harder than I thought it would be.

"Mami, I'm sorry I disappointed you. I was careless. Again. If you want to send me back to Nana Sherry, I understand."

Mami's eyebrow lowered into her I'll-think-about-it face. She looked at Papa.

"I don't know…" Mami said. "What do you think, Doc B?"

"Well, Dr. Baxter…" Papa said, "sounds like someone's first day of school started with a pop quiz on actions and consequences." He smiled and gave me a wink.

Hic!

"Aww, mi corazón," Mami whispered in my ear. "Also sounds like someone's been crying."

I nodded. She patted my cheek.

"It's okay. We'll talk later."

Mami turned to her boss. "Commander Johansson, thank you for helping the children find their way back here. It was exceedingly kind of you, and we won't forget your benevolence."

The other parents agreed.

"My pleasure, Dr. Baxter. Now…" The commander looked around the room. "I'm sure we all have work to return to, so let's get to it."

The grown-ups headed to the door. Then Commander Johansson stopped and turned to me.

"Abigail Baxter, can you tell me what you learned today—"

Before I could open my mouth, she raised one finger.

"In *one* word only?" she continued.

"Teamwork," I said.

The commander nodded. She even smiled a little. Then—

Hic! HIC!

"Hold your breath and count to thirty," the commander said before she disappeared through the door.

"You heard Commander Johansson, children," Mr. Krishna said to the whole class.

"Okay!" The Level 1 kids puffed out their cheeks to hold their breath for thirty seconds.

"No," Mr. Krishna replied with a sigh, "we need to return to our lessons. All levels back to your stations."

After all that, we'd only been gone for about twenty minutes. It was still exercise period for Level 2, but Mr. Krishna said we'd had enough excitement for the day. So instead of playing a virtual reality game, we had to read the class rules. Gracie and Dmitry hopped onto their exercise bikes, strapped themselves in, and got to work. I floated over, pulled out my tablet, and joined them.

"Are your parents mad at you?" I asked. They both nodded.

"Are you mad at me?"

Gracie looked down, like she was avoiding me. Dmitry looked up, like he was thinking.

"We should not have done what we did," Gracie said. Then a huge grin lit up her face. "But it was so much fun!" She quickly covered her smile with her hand.

"The beginning of the mission was poorly planned, and the end was a disaster," Dmitry said with a scowl. "But the middle? Interstellar."

"Interstellar!" Gracie replied.

It was only the first day of school, but I knew it right then. Level 2 was going to be the best team in the class, on the OASIS, in the solar system, the Milky Way galaxy, the whole universe, and possibly the multiverse!

But I couldn't shout it out loud, so I had to say it quietly.

"Inter—*hic*—stellar," I whispered, smiling.

Dmitry put on his earphones. "That is so very annoying."

CHAPTER 9

Between the Seas
and the Stars

In the end, it turned out to be a pretty good
day for the Baxters of the OASIS International
Space Station. Mami's big experiment went
better than she thought it would—even
Commander Johansson was impressed. Nico
and his new friends learned how to say "hello"
in five languages. And Papa's laughter filled
the whole pod as he listened to the story of my
big adventure.

Still, Mami said that sneaking around the OASIS had consequences. So after school I had to write an apology to Mr. Krishna, Commander Johansson, and every single one of the 135 people on the space station. It took a while to type it all, but I felt 200 percent better after I hit that last Send.

"Good," Mami said as she handed me some wipes. "Next, when your brother's finally done, you can clean the bathroom."

Cheese and craters! Nico tried his best, but used wipes, stinky blobs of pee, and little hand-prints were everywhere. What a mess!

After I finished scrubbing everything, Mami said, "Abby, let's take a break."

Mami opened the door to the busy Main Pod. The sound of people talking roared all around us. But now it didn't seem so scary and confusing. I could see the streams of traffic to the different doors. I even saw the door to the One Pod Schoolhouse.

"This place takes a little getting used to," Mami said. "And you know that's okay, Abby. We're learning something new. We're going to make mistakes."

"You don't make mistakes, Mami."

My mother smiled. Then she opened the next door.

"Do you want to hear a secret, Abby?"

We entered the corridor, and the door *shuuushed* closed behind us.

"You didn't switch those tablets," Mami said. "I did. I was so busy thinking about work and you and your brother...when we left this morning, I just grabbed the first tablet I saw. Turns out it was yours. I'm sorry, Abby."

Wait! It was *Mami* who took *my* tablet? It wasn't all my fault after all? Suddenly I felt 300 percent better about everything. But that dropped to 150 percent when I remembered all my mistakes.

"It's okay, Mami."

"I've never had an eight-year-old daughter before. I still have a lot to learn."

"I've never been eight before! I have so many things to learn. Especially here."

Mami smiled at me.

"So let's make a deal. I'll learn how to be more patient with you, and you'll learn how to be more patient with me."

"It's a deal!" I said.

"We're here," Mami said, pulling me down.

"This is the cupola. It's a special observation pod."

The cupola was like a huge glass bubble hanging from the bottom of the space station. Mami and I squeezed inside. Then I sat on her lap.

Through the window was the biggest, bluest, swirliest, most magnificent thing I'd ever seen.

Planet Earth.

"Wow!" I couldn't take my eyes off our home planet. I could see it all—oceans, mountain ranges, storm clouds...everything. It was eleventy-seventy-infinity kinds of cool.

"Pretty amazing, huh?" Mami said. "When I first came here, do you know what I thought?"

"You thought about how beautiful Earth is?"

"I thought about you, Abby. How you would love being able to see everything on the planet at the same time. I thought about this moment we're having right now."

"Really?" My mother's brain was always so full of science and theories and rules and stuff I didn't understand. Sometimes I forgot that I was in there too.

I gave my mother the biggest, squeeziest hug.

"Ah, and there it is!" she said. We watched the sun light up the middle of the United States.

"There's your Nana Sherry's house."

I waved to Nana Sherry, even though I knew she and her little dog couldn't see us. I waved to everyone in Houston and Texas and the United States and the Americas and the whole world.

Then I thought about all the people on the OASIS—the ones I'd met and the ones I had yet to meet. I thought about all the people on missions and spaceships and stations on the moon and Mars and even beyond.

"We're right in the middle of everything and everyone, aren't we, Mami?"

"We are between the seas and the stars, mi corazón."

"We've got the best spot in the universe," I said.

My mother hugged me closer.

"That's why we're here together. No one's going back to Houston right now. Even if we make mistakes, we'll figure it out as a family."

Those words were all I'd wanted to hear all day long. I felt 1000 percent better.

Mami and I watched Earth whirl by for a long, long time.

It was out of this world.

It was interstellar.

Abby's Vocabulary

baba: Mandarin Chinese for "daddy"

da: Russian for "yes"

interstellar: Between the stars

mi corazón: Spanish for "my heart" or "my sweetheart"

microgravity: Gravity forces smaller than Earth's

mira: Spanish for "look"

nyet: Russian for "no"

orbit: Movement on a curved path around something (like the moon circling Earth)

vamos: Spanish for "let's go!"

Abby's Orbital Observations

(Real Science for Kids Way Back in the 2020s)

Emergencies in Space

Just like you have emergency drills in school on Earth, there are safety drills on the real space station too. Sometimes solar flares from the sun, fires, or toxic leaks put the people on the station in danger. So alarms sound and astronauts move to a protected area in the station until the danger passes or they fix the problem.

Working Up, Down, and All Around

Astronauts use all the surfaces of a pod—the floors, the ceilings, and the walls. A space station has to fit a lot of activities in a tiny space. And without gravity, there's no need to stay on the floor.

The International Space Station

The original ISS has been orbiting the earth sixteen times a day since 2000. But it only holds six people at a time. You can check NASA's website to see when it might fly over your town.

It's time for the first ever OASIS Space Race, a virtual reality obstacle course designed to make space's required exercise fun. Abby and her classmate Dmitry both want to win for their age group, so much so that they don't pay attention to the rules and accidentally get stuck in the simulation, glitching their friend Gracie's designs. If they want to find a way out, they're going to have to work together.

Space Race
978-0-8075-0097-2 • US $13.99
Hardcover available September 2022
Book 3 coming Spring 2023

Award-winning author **Andrea J. Loney** grew up in a small town in New Jersey. After receiving her MFA from New York University, she joined a traveling circus, then stayed in Hollywood to make movies. Now Andrea teaches computer classes at a community college while living in Los Angeles with her family and their embarrassingly spoiled pets. Learn more at andreajloney.com.

Once a professional nurse, **Fuuji Takashi** is now a children's book illustrator and character designer from General Santos, Philippines. She is best known for illustrating Kailyn Lowry's first children's book, *Love Is Bubblegum,* and for her work on children's books featuring diverse characters. In her spare time, she likes singing, cooking, and taking long, peaceful walks.